No Help Wanted!

Ruth Ohi

North Winds Press

An Imprint of Scholastic Canada Ltd.

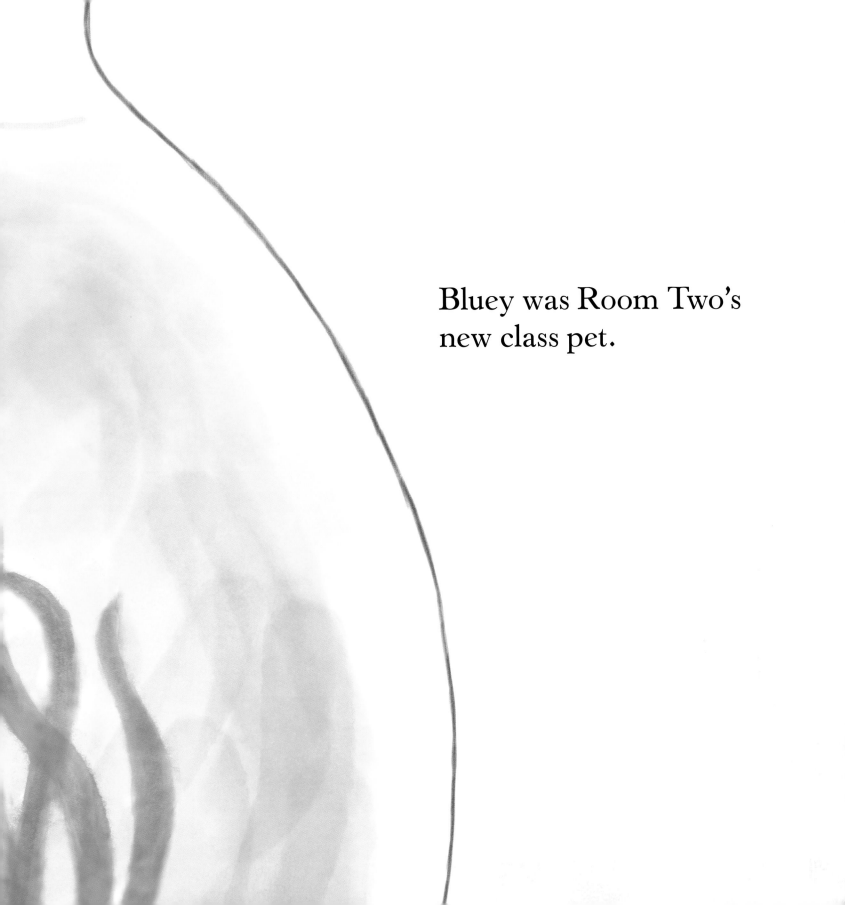

Bluey was Room Two's
new class pet.

Mr. Zen talked about how someone needed to feed Bluey every day.

Posy was very keen.

Posy picked the fanciest food
flakes for Bluey.

Posy provided stimulation
so Bluey was never bored.

"We can all be friends!" growled Posy
in her best Monster Shark voice.

The following day, Jacob said, "I made
a puppet too."

"I'll take that!" said Posy. "This will help with the parade scene."

"I think Bluey needs a checkup," said
Sam. "I'm a vet. May I take a look?"

"I'll do it," said Posy.
"You'll scare her."

"All you need is me," said Posy.

But Bluey was not looking
that well.

Posy formed
each food flake
into a tiny tiara.

But Bluey was not impressed.

The next day, Posy staged a full-scale, fish-themed musical.

But still Bluey looked
unwell.

"Everyone will blame me!"
thought Posy.

So Posy hid Bluey.

But Bluey was
not napping.

BLUEY?!!!

Oh no.

Posy knew what she had to do.

The class came
and helped.

Bluey started looking better.

So did Posy.

"You are a great fish friend," said Mr. Zen. "Thanks for letting us help."

The following week was Jacob's turn.
Posy had lots of helpful tips.

And the class couldn't help noticing
that Bluey always seemed to enjoy. . .

. . . a good puppet show.

For Hewitt, Alexandra, Maeve,
Charlie and Ian

Library and Archives Canada Cataloguing in Publication

Ohi, Ruth, author, illustrator
No help wanted! / [written and illustrated by] Ruth Ohi.

Published simultaneously in softcover by Scholastic Canada Ltd.
ISBN 978-1-4431-6360-6 (hardcover)

I. Title.

PS8579.H47N6 2019   jC813'.6   C2018-906334-3

www.scholastic.ca

Author photo by Annie T.

6 5 4 3 2 1   Printed in Malaysia 108   19 20 21 22 23 24